ERIC CARLE FRIENDS

PUFFIN

Once there were two friends who were always together.

Together they played

and ran

ERIC CARLE
FRIENDS

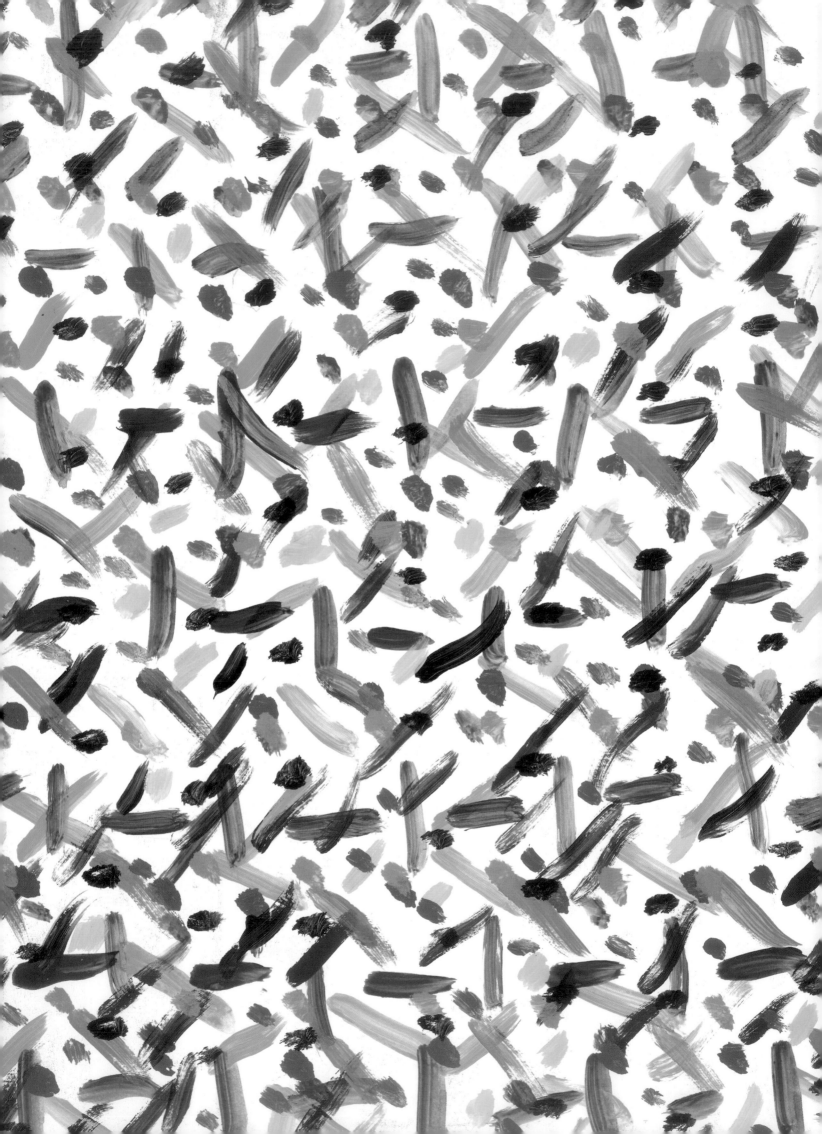

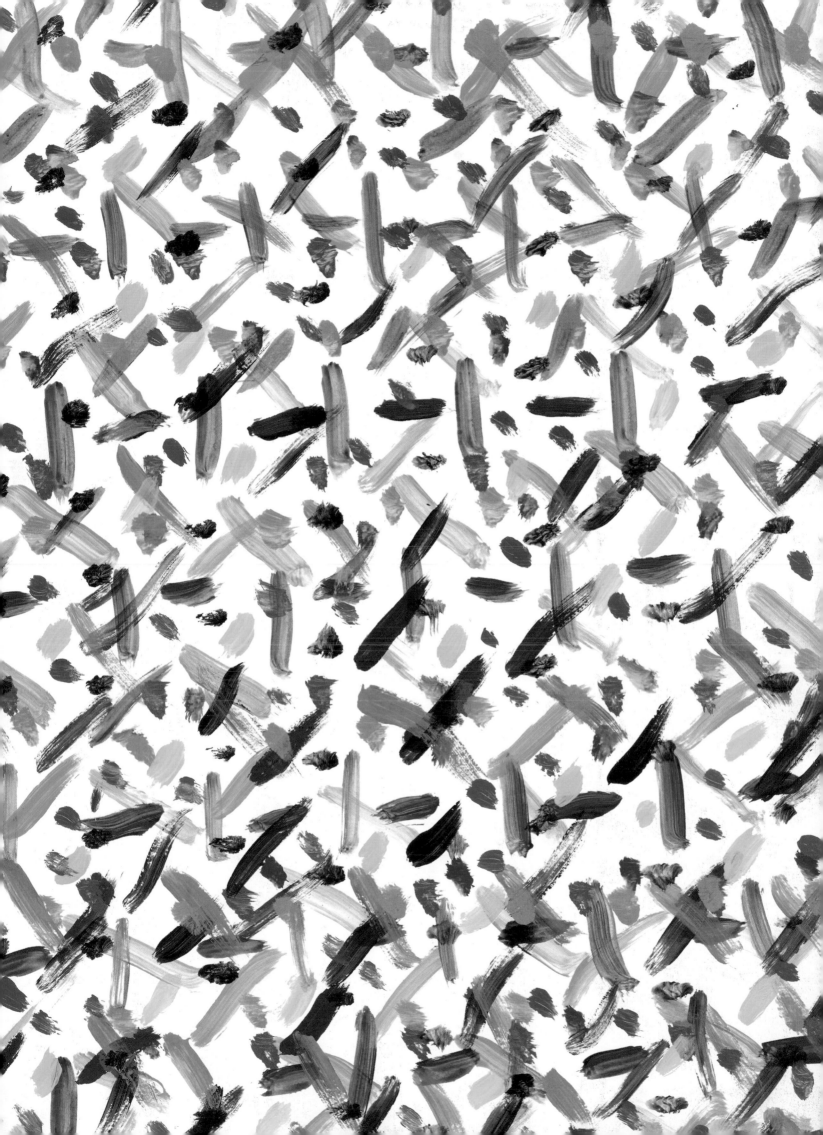

For Bobbie

PUFFIN BOOKS

Published by the Penguin Group: London, New York, Australia, Canada, India, Ireland,
New Zealand and South Africa
Penguin Books Ltd, Registered Offices: 80 Strand, London WC2R 0RL, England
puffinbooks.com

First published in the USA by Philomel Books, an imprint of Penguin Young Readers Group, 2013
Published simultaneously in Great Britain by Puffin Books 2013
This edition published 2015
001

The text is set in 32-point Walbaum Com

The art was created with painted tissue-paper collage

Made and printed in China

ISBN: 978–0–723–29593–8

Eric Carle's name and his signature logotype are trademarks of Eric Carle.
To learn more about Eric Carle, please visit *eric-carle.com*
To learn about The Eric Carle Museum of Picture Book Art, please visit *carlemuseum.org*

and danced

and told each other secrets.

But one day, the boy was all alone. His friend was gone.
She had moved far away.
"I miss her," he said.
"Wherever she is, I must find her."

Then he took a deep breath,
counted to ten, and . . .

. . . jumped into the swift river. The water was cold. *B-r-r-r!*

The river was wide, so it took a long time to swim across it.

When he got to the other side, it was already dark.

The stars watched over him as he fell asleep. *Z-z-z-z.*

The next morning, he saw a tall mountain ahead.
He started up one side of it. The path was steep.

It was hard work. Finally he got to the top, and then . . .
he slid right down the other side. *Plunk!*

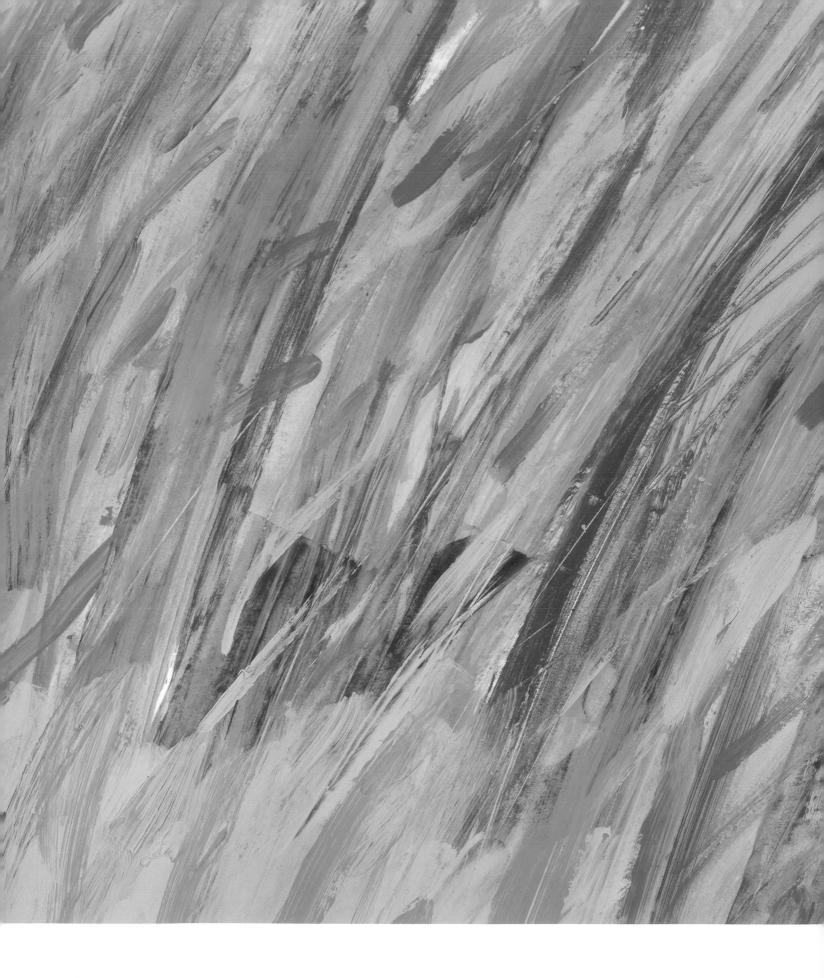

The boy landed in a broad meadow. It was a hot day.
The grass was dewy, damp and cool.

He strolled through it. *A-h-h-h.*

Then, all of a sudden, it began to rain. *Splish! Splash!*

He had to dash through the falling drops.

After a while, the boy felt tired. He fell asleep

and dreamed that he was floating on a cloud. *M-m-m-m.*

He woke up deep in a forest.
Dark shadows danced around him.

E-e-e-k! He rushed out of the woods into . . .

. . . a flower garden.

He gathered a bouquet.

And there was his friend!

"I have found you!" he shouted.
"I knew you would come," she said.

Together they played
and ran
and danced
and told each other secrets . . .

. . . and got married.

Juni 1932

Here I am with a friend in Syracuse, New York.
I was three years old and so was she.
My German mother took this picture.
She wrote *Juni* (June) *1932* in the corner.

When I was six, I moved far away.
We never saw each other again.
I often think about my long-ago friend,
and I wonder what happened to her.

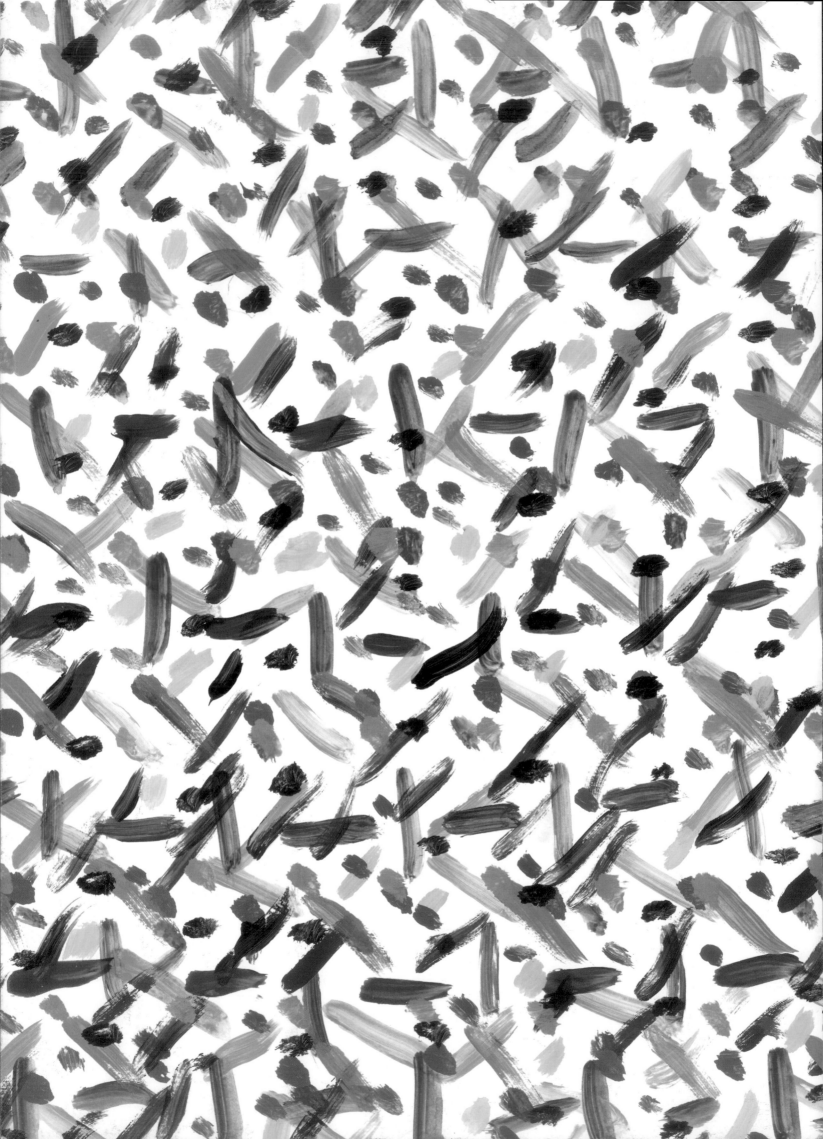

★ OTHER TITLES BY ERIC CARLE ★

Board Book
9780141357430

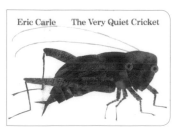

Board Book
9780241137857

Paperback
9780141348131

Paperback
9780141338323

Paperback
9780140569322

Paperback
9780141332031

Paperback
9780140502848

Paperback
9780140506426

Paperback
9780140569896

Paperback
9780140509267

Paperback
9780140556780

Paperback
9780140569247

Paperback
9780140563788

Paperback
9780140557138

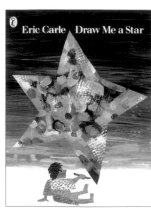

Paperback
9780140549270

Paperback
9780140562781

Paperback
9780140553109